THE WASTREL AND THE Wallflower

ELIANA PIERS

The Wastrel and the Wallflower is a work of fiction. Names, characters, places, and incidents are the products of the author's imagination or are used fictitiously. Any resemblance to actual events, locales, or persons, living or dead, is entirely coincidental.

ISBN E-Book 978-1-998281-23-7
ISBN Print 978-1-998281-24-4

ISBN Audio 978-1-998281-25-1

Dedication

To all y'all who, when asked the question, "Do you think you are beautiful?" hesitate to say yes.

Know this:

The answer is yes! Yes, you are beautiful.

Free E-book

Get my **FREE** Short Story when you sign up to join my mailing list. Plus you'll learn more about me, get sneak peeks at what's in the works, as well as receive access to some discounted or free books from other authors.

Sweeten the Rogue: One wager, one evening of passion, two possible futures for a rogue and a lady

Or use this link here to receive the free ebook: https://bit.ly/SweetenTheRogue

Or email me to get the story: elianapiers@gmail.com

Contents

Author's Note

Hello Beautiful Reader,

Welcome to the Beau Monde. Most, if not all, of my books are part of an interconnected world with the Good Dukes, where it all started. This series, The Ashbourne Legacy follows the 7 brothers of Snow White, and it has some enchanting fairytale vibes for you.

If you like SHORT, SWEET & SPICY, you are in for a treat.

I love to write funny, easy, breezy stories where the characters learn things about themselves and the world around them, all the while continuing to reach for hope, joy, and above all, LOVE.

Love always wins. Love never fails.

You will always read a happy ending in my stories.

I write to have fun, and so I make stories fit into a historical context, but I often take leeway with history. SO, if you are looking for a 100% accurate depiction of historical language and settings, please put this book down. You will be disappointed. And I don't want that. You don't want that. Neither of us wants you to be disappointed. Let's just be happy. The world is a hard enough place as it is.

IF, however, you don't mind to sacrifice some historical truths in the name of LOVE and HUMOR, AND you want to read about some HOT men falling head over heels in love with some INTELLIGENT, STRONG, INDEPENDENT women, then read on, dear reader.

Much love,

Eliana Piers

Chapter 1

1816 England

One day earlier

WITH A REASONABLE DEGREE of certainty and enjoyment, Giselle would often make predictions. How many people would attend a house party. Who would be the life of the party. What jokes would be made. Who would laugh. Who would fake laugh. Whose heads the joke would fly over.

Her success rate at predicting events of the social realm were just slightly above average. Or perhaps, just average.

The only truly successful predictions she could make about society related to the male species. That is, she predicted with perfect accuracy, that handsome men would not dance with her, speak to her, and rarely (if ever) would they even notice her.

Of course, such a prediction could be made by many others in the *ton.* After all, she was a wallflower for a reason.

Giselle accepted her fate. She didn't even mind it so much. She enjoyed time to herself and her thoughts. The less men spoke with her, the more time she could spend planning her next day's tasks.

And the next day's tasks almost always involved the weather. Which, to say the least, Giselle was also very good at predicting.

Predictions, predictions, predictions. It was all about looking at past evidence, analyzing data, noting patterns, crafting a reasonable conclusion, and the forecasting that the future would follow suit.

It was the way of the world. People didn't change all that much. Humanity as a whole didn't change all that much. Science didn't change all that much. Though many might be tempted to refute that statement, the truth was that science was science, only its discovery and application changed. The world worked the way the world worked.

Gravity didn't start acting up only once Newton observed the apple. No. Gravity had always been in full force. One day someone finally noticed it.

The same could be said of the sun, the stars, the ocean. Animals. Anything and everything science covered, was either discovered or waiting to be uncovered.

And that about covered it.

People could be a bit more fickle. Fashion changed. Language changed. Culture changed. It was a bit more challenging to keep up with it all. The weight of those trivial matters could weigh on Giselle's mind if she wasn't careful. And conscientious. She had to always remind herself of her limitations. Another such limitation was her options for marriage.

An arranged marriage, or a marriage of convenience was well within her reach. And it was a good reach. There were worse cases. Scandal. Ruination. Spinsterhood. Horrible husbands. Absent husbands.

She shuddered. If nothing else, there were two things she didn't want: one, to be completely alone, or two, dependent upon family for her future wellbeing.

Her plan was to allow her parents to select her mate. They had given her a few seasons to try and find a love match, which Giselle had successfully predicted was impossible, and this summer was her last summer to be single. Next year her parents would make her a match. She was...comfortable with that. Content. Certainly not excited, giddy, or blushing about her future prospects. But that kind of behavior was for young girls anyway. She was a mature woman of three-and-twenty.

She was well beyond the erratic butterflies and sweaty palms. Though...could one really say one was beyond it when one had never experienced it? Not even once?

These were the multitude of thoughts flashing through Giselle's mind as she sipped tea among company.

The ladies around her were chattering and smiling blithely. One was blushing. She suspected that if anyone had a reason to blush, it was Emma. She had just gotten engaged to Dawson. Right beside Emma was Della who was bearing the largest grin on her face. Giselle sighed. If anyone had a reason to grin, it was Della. She had just gotten engaged to Colin.

"Four engagements, Mother," Hope said in awe. "I can't believe it."

Giselle noticed that Hope had a smirk on her face, but she couldn't quite interpret it.

Hope's mother patted her daughter's hand. "Four sons all betrothed. Perhaps we shall have a large fourway wedding at the end of summer to marry everyone off."

"There's still time," Della chimed in. "There might be more."

In mirth, Mavis shook her head, "I should love for all seven of my sons to marry, but mostly I just want them to be happy."

"And what of your daughter?" Hope asked archly. "Do you want her to marry and be happy as well?"

"Of course, my dear. You are the last one though. It might be harder to see you married than all seven boys."

The ladies in the room chuckled.

"I'm sure if we all worked together, we could get all your sons married off this summer," suggested Emma, one of the future daughters-in-law.

"It's true. And it would be quite simple. Men are so predictable. They fall in love quicker than we women do." Hope smiled.

Giselle's head perked up. *Men are so predictable?* She only knew one thing to predict about men, and it wouldn't help in getting a ring on her finger.

"All you have to do is dangle something pretty in front of them..." Hope paused until all eyes were on her.

Giselle's heart thundered in her chest. Was there hope? Was there some prediction, some male science, that she was yet aware of that could guarantee a love match? At least one-way?

Hope repeated her earlier phrase and sailed on. "All you have to do...is put something pretty in front of them and then tell them they can't have it."

She released the breath she had been holding. If only Hope had held a helpful secret to the inner workings of the male species, then Giselle would latch onto it. But this reveal was impossible to claim because if that was what it took, Giselle was a lost cause.

She was a seven at best. Out of ten. Oh, she knew her number. The number had somehow been the whispered *on dit*, on more than one occasion. Seven was decent. It meant that at least she had been noticed. Except...from all her scientific data gathering and analysis, seven out of ten was a terrible number to receive. It meant precisely what she hoped it couldn't mean. Seven meant that the object being rated wasn't worth the attention to rate it. Slap a seven on it and move on.

Anything less than a seven was plain. Or less than plain. She couldn't even bring herself to say anything more demeaning than that. So, yes, a seven...nothing worth noting. There was that.

The ladies were chatting again, and Giselle glanced out the window. It was another sunny day. She didn't want to waste the whole afternoon sitting inside when she could be outside taking notes. Taking note of things that mattered. She would get outside for a walk immediately after tea, of that she was determined.

She felt a small nudge at her side.

"What about you?" Hope smiled up at her. "Have you set your cap on someone?"

"No. No caps for me to set. It would be just my luck to set my cap for someone and he return it to the wrong owner."

Hope giggled. "Giselle, you are too funny. Any man would be lucky to have you."

Giselle grimaced. "That's a...nice thought." That kind of compliment didn't make sense to her. She hardly believed there was *any* man that would enjoy her company, never mind the idea that every man was a possibility.

"You have so much to offer, including your intellect."

That's what people said to someone who was a seven. "Men don't want to be around an intelligent woman. Especially one who's smarter than they are." It was a fact. Not arrogance. She was smarter than many men, and whenever a man discovered how deep her knowledge went, they went away. And by *they*, Giselle meant the handful of men her mother had (blackmailed?) into talking to her.

"Some men love smart women."

"But all men love beautiful women." She couldn't suppress it. It was a knee jerk reaction.

"Exactly," Hope beamed another smile at her. It didn't seem to be a patronizing smile. It seemed to be genuine. But no one had ever called Giselle beautiful before. Intelligent? Yes. Determined? Yes. Productive? Always. Odd? Sometimes. Daughter of an earl with an average dowry? Yes. Beautiful? No.

It just wasn't done. And based on Giselle's thorough understanding of data and patterns, it was not likely for someone to call her beautiful in the future. And she was content knowing that.

Mostly.

Chapter 2

IT WAS A BEAUTIFUL day for kite flying, Lord Felix's favorite pastime. Was it childish? He didn't care. Some people thought it a waste of a day to fly a kite. He thought it a waste of a kite not to.

The wind was blowing. The sun was out, and by God, he was going to enjoy this afternoon.

He took another step in line with Giles, his youngest brother. "Are you sure you don't want to join me?"

Giles gave him a look. Eyebrow to the sky said it all. Or it would have, but Giles wanted to further elucidate Felix. "I have some adult tasks to accomplish this afternoon. Unlike some people."

"*Adult* tasks?" Felix laughed. "Well, now I understand completely. if you had said that the first time I had asked, I would have let you be."

"Not those kinds of tasks, you bacon brain. Just...other things that adults do." Giles looked frustrated. He looked as though he were holding in some secrets. And not the good kind that a person could share.

"It's all right. Go ahead, and do your *adult* things." Felix couldn't keep the chuckle of his voice. He rarely could. Life was too short to take it too seriously. "Wait. You're not off to propose, are you?"

Giles choked on the air in front of him. "Propose? What the devil are you talking about?"

"You might be feeling the itch."

"The itch?" he asked cagily.

"For the love of love, man, haven't you noticed our brothers dropping like flies?"

"Oh, yes. That."

Felix tucked his packaged kite under his arm and started counting digits. "Arthur, Barnaby, Colin, Dawson. All four ready to tie the knot." Giles wasn't getting it, so Felix amped up his speech. "This summer." And because that wasn't enough, "They're all going to be married by the end of the summer. Not a one of them is waiting."

"Yes."

"That's all you have to say."

"Based on what you just said, I still have some time to dodge whatever is floating about."

"I doubt it. If Dawson fell, I don't see what hope there is for the rest of us."

Giles grumbled inarticulately.

"Your eloquence eludes me."

"I was just saying that we should wait to see what happens with Evan."

"You think he's the tougher nut to crack? He's just overworked. He might be the one who needs a wife the most."

"Perhaps. But just because he needs a wife, doesn't mean he will fall in love."

"Well, would you look at that? Aren't you the romantic, Giles? I didn't know you had it in you. All that love."

The taunt was received with an expected harrumph. Exactly what Felix would have predicted, if he were the type to make predictions. Which he really wasn't.

"Giles, I know you're a man of few words, and your resting face is more serious than most, but even for you, you seem a bit more sullen than normal. Something on your mind, man?"

"You could say that."

"I just did. Do you want to tell me what it is?"

Giles shoved his hands in his pockets. "I almost might want to." The pause wasn't quite long enough for Felix to jump in. "But I can't say anything."

"Well, now. That makes things interesting." Felix rubbed his hands together, tightly holding the package still under his armpit. "You can't say anything because either you don't know how to say it..." Felix stalled, waiting for a reaction. ""Or you're bound to secrecy." And there it was. A tiny shift on Giles face.

"A secret it is."

"Do you ever find yourself obliged to do something you don't really want to do?"

"I don't think a person can claim maturity until they frequently accept that life is full of doing things we don't want to do."

"Probably true."

"But there are different kinds of wants. We can want something but not want to do what it takes to achieve that. For example, we can want to make money but not want to put in the time and effort. Inversely, we can want to do something but not want the known outcome. For example, we can want to have a few drinks, but not want the hangover. See what I mean? Different kinds of wants. What kind of want are you talking about?"

"The former."

"Then it's worth it. Whatever it is. Just do it."

"Wise words, Felix."

"Yes. Well, I'm chock full of it. Are you going to tell me what it is now?"

Giles stopped walking. "Don't press me for this one, Felix." The glint in his eye was serious enough to make Felix question the benefit in pushing for more details.

"At least you don't have the day to day ennui the rest of us have."

"You? Ennui? I didn't think it possible." Giles took up their former pace.

"I didn't think it possible either. But lately...there's just something missing," Felix lightly snapped his fingers a few times. Not the kind of snap someone does when they've just experienced enlightenment. More the kind of snap someone does repeatedly in hopes of triggering some kind of enlightenment. "I can't put my finger on it though."

"Maybe it's a wife." Giles cracked a smile.

"Ha ha. Joke or not, you very well could be onto something there. I guess if I'm patient and wait my turn, fate might already have that lined up for me."

"Ever the optimist."

"I can't help it."

"Nor should you." Giles patted him on the back. "I'm off to the house. I really ought to be putting more effort into that task I have."

Felix rubbed his hands together again, this time in a circular motion, the universal gesture to convey his villainous plotting. "You have presented me with a moral dilemma. Now that I know what you're about to do, should I follow you and try to glean more details into my younger brother's life? Or...should I–"

"Go fly a kite, Felix."

Chapter 3

THERE WAS SOMETHING ABOUT flying a kite that opened Felix's mind to dream. Maybe it was the open sky. Free and clear. Wide. Waiting. An open space. A blank canvas. The mind could roam in such a space.

Maybe it was the wind. It came in and blew out old ideas, old ways of thinking. If one never rid themselves of the old, there was no space for the new to enter.

Maybe it was the simple act of flying a kite itself. It took little thought. It offered endless fascination and pleasure. And...well, there was just something about hanging onto something that wanted to be free.

That's the way it was with thoughts. Ideas and people were similar in their desire for freedom. But if freedom was defined as being able to do whatever one wanted whenever one wanted to do it, then that wasn't true freedom for everyone. Freedom had to have limits. It was completely counterintuitive, but without limits, one person's freedom could infringe, or even violate, another person's freedom.

There was freedom to do things, and there was freedom from things. Freedom to speak and think and act how one wanted was one type of freedom. Freedom from violence, harm, abuse was another kind of freedom.

Kites epitomized the give and take of freedom.

Yet they were child's play.

Felix felt the draw to fly his kite, and he knew just where he wanted to do so. The pond was the most scenic place he could think of. There he could allow his thoughts to randomly populate ideas, perhaps thinking of a way to break the ennui. And if he just bided his time, maybe a wife was the answer. And maybe fate was ready for him. He just needed to ready himself. And be patient. Because if anything was true about fate, it seemed to be working in a nice orderly pattern. And up next was Evan.

He didn't think there was too much preparation to do. He believed himself quite open to love, having claimed to be in love on more than one occasion. It wasn't enough for him to fall for a pretty face though, the pretty face always had to have a pretty soul to match. His heart was open. His eyes were open. He just...wasn't sure what to do with his time.

His brothers were preoccupied with the family's mines or something indirectly related to the mines. Like animal rescue and safety, healthy and safety for the miners, fighting for better child labor laws, rescuing children from exploitative work environments, the secret orphanage to improve those children's lives. And so much more. The Ashbournes had been successfully managing the mines and the projects indirectly related to the mines. Felix played a small role, from time to time, but not to the same extent as any of the other family members. But he would come up with something. He'd find his place. Soon. He wasn't worried. Too much.

As he came closer to the pond, he surveyed his surroundings. Scouting the perfect place to fly his kite, his eyes rested on a figure in the distance. She was leaning against a tree trunk. She almost looked as though she were hiding, which was patently ridiculous to think since no one was around. Not even without shouting distance.

If she was hiding, he wanted to know why. Also ridiculous to think, since if she was hiding, she probably didn't want someone trying to find her. Though...not everyone hiding wanted to remain hidden...

Those obscure thoughts drew Felix to, rather than deter him from, the lady under the tree. She wasn't paying any attention to him as he walked near the pond's perimeter. She was gazing at the sky, and every so often she would jot down some notes in her book.

All he could see was her profile. And he was enjoying it immensely. She had a delicate jaw and soft pink lips. Perhaps he imagined the soft pink color. He was still over ten paces away. But the brilliant blonde waves with a silky sheen was not imagined. It was the most glorious hair he had ever seen. If her profile was half as gorgeous as he imagined her full face, which, by definition it was, *she* was the most glorious woman he had ever seen. He just needed to get closer and view her full face. The prospect of such surged through him. His neck was craned to see her. There was a weightlessness in his limbs. It made him feel as though he could be a kite and soar up and over to her. It was unnatural and pure bliss. There was even a lightness in his next step. It was unnatural but a sure miss.

His weightless foot did not land on the soft first path he had been traversing. No. It landed on the soft slippery bank of the pond. He threw his package to his left, away from the water. *Save the kite!* was his last thought before...

SPLASH!

***

GISELLE HAD BEEN EYEING the man who was walking toward her. She didn't want him to see her in particular. Though, she didn't *not* want him to see her either...per se. But he was staring at her as if she were the only woman he had ever seen. True, she was the only woman for at least a mile, but really, did he need to stare?

And then, through the corner of her eye, she saw him watching her as he slipped down into the pond.

What a buffoon.

She rolled her eyes. Had the poor sod been drinking? What could possibly have caused him to be so distracted by her that he would fall into the pond? Should she get up? She wasn't sure. She didn't really want to... but she didn't *not* want to either...per se.

She got up.

Placing her book and barometer near the tree trunk, she smoothed her skirts and meandered over to the pond to offer some assistance.

When she reached the pond's edge, she saw the man, truly saw him (at least part of him), for the first time. It was just a hand.

He was sluicing the water from his face with a giant palm. A hand had never looked so...sensual before. It was a large hand, large enough to hold the weight of her increasingly weighty breasts. When did breasts react to seeing a hand before? Giselle could feel an immediate heat penetrating her frock. Must be the sun.

The man raked his hands through his hair, revealing his face. The most handsome face she had ever seen. This man was a ten. If she were rating men. Which she didn't do. That was childish and rude. All the same, he would have been a ten.

He had piercing blue eyes, eyes that pierced with a ray of sunshine, not a sword. Eyes that saw quickly, happily, and nonjudgmentally. He had an openness about him that was just altogether unnerving. She had never seen a person with such an openness about them. And then he shocked her nervous system.

He grinned.

Perfect teeth. Gorgeous smile. At her. For no known reason.

Her eyebrows drew down together toward her nose. Despite her obvious scowl, the man called out cheerily, "Hello."

Oh, that voice. It sank into her bones. No, it covered her bones, dripping with honey. It did both in the reverse order. God, how could a voice be so...smooth?

But he was just being polite. He hadn't reserved that voice for her. So, in order to move things along in the way she knew such events would unfold (though truthfully, what evidence did she possess regarding wet men?), she replied, "Do you need help? Or can I go back to my business?"

He belted out a laugh. She felt dwarfed in his presence. By his sheer size, but also the size and enveloping nature of his laugh.

It was...charming. But she couldn't allow herself to be charmed by this man. This wet man. He was wet. Truly soaked. Wet. And. Saked. What were those words doing to her?

Then she did the worst thing she could have possibly done in that moment. She looked down. And she could see the shape of things in his breeches. She had never looked before. Well, of course she had *looked*. But she had never studied before. Oh who was she kidding, she had studied, as discreetly as she could.

But in this moment she not only studied, she indulged. And indulging in the bulge she could see in his breeches caused a swell between her legs that most certainly had never happened before.

She clenched her bottom, and her thighs, and asked again, "Do you need help?"

"I'm fine," he said through his smile that was wider than the pond he was wading in. He took a step, trudging through what must be layers of sludge in the pond. He was advancing, albeit slowly. When he reached the bank, he looked up at her. Why hadn't she left yet? Had she forgotten his answer? He said he was fine. That meant he didn't need her help. That meant she could have left him and gone back to her notes.

His honey sweet voice rang out, "On second thought..."

Chapter 4

HE WAS THE MOST beautiful man she had ever seen. If one could call a man beautiful. She was pretty sure she was thinking it merely as a scientific fact. Purely observational. If anyone was good at observing, it was Giselle.

"On second thought, I could use some help." Putting a foot on the bank, he reached out his arm, essentially asking for a hand up. It didn't look as though he needed it. The bank was shallow enough for him to get out on his own. Why was he asking for help?

Without a word (because she hoped her dubious expression said it all), she put her hand out for him to grab.

The touch was magnetic. It drew closed without effort. Like they were meant to be held. She was holding those large hands. With long, smooth fingers. Large knuckles. Soft, yet masculine. She wondered what else those hands could hold.

A shiver ran between her shoulder blades and down each arm. Something about this man unnerved her. Their hands clasped, he pulled himself out of the water. She did nothing really. Just observed. Which...really...that was her thing.

"What are you doing out here?"

Men didn't make conversation with Giselle. Especially not handsome men. And most especially not dripping wet men with godlike bodies. Or so she figured. The fabric was clinging to him. His every muscle. And then some. "What, I can't be out here on my own?"

He chuckled. "I didn't say that."

"But you were thinking it."

"Actually, no. I was just making conversation."

It was time to point out the obvious. Apparently this man didn't know how things were supposed to work. "Men like you don't make conversation with ladies like me."

His smile vanished, and his eyebrows drew together. In cahoots of some sort. What was he thinking?

"And...what kind of man am I?"

"You're..." what could she say? Handsome? Gorgeous? The reddest apple ever depicted to Eve? "You're...you look like you."

He waited.

The nerve of him. Making her explain what should be obvious. Perhaps he was a special kind of handsome devil. The kind that wasted away his thoughts and only let others provide ideas to him.

"And I'm me."

"You?"

"Yes."

"I'm me, and you're you."

"Exactly." That should be clear enough. She didn't actually have to say it, did she?

He shook his head and some water droplets landed on her cheek. Why was there an increasingly large portion of her that wanted to leave the water droplets where they lay? Wanted to let them soak into her skin. Wanted to let them stain her cheek, if only to have had more contact with him.

She was being ridiculous.

"Please explain."

"I'm a wallflower, for God's sake. Are you happy now?"

"Yes?" He sliced his fingers through his hair again. "I think that should be the correct answer, but I have the strangest feeling that you will think it is the wrong answer. Am I right?"

Wait. What? She couldn't think straight.

With a smile, he established his position. Which is to say, she couldn't counter the argument because she was temporarily blinded by the radiance of his teeth. Since when did blindness affect cognitive abilities? Since now. In the presence of such luminescence.

"May I join you?"

She couldn't have declined if she wanted to. And she wasn't sure she wanted to.

The radiance led her onward. A few steps in, he grabbed a small package, and then he strolled the rest of the way to the tree she had been sitting under.

Placing the package on the grass, he proceeded to take off his dripping wet jacket. "I'll just let that dry out a bit."

Her tongue had dried out a bit.

And now he was rolling up his sleeves. Was he actually about to untie his cravat? He wouldn't–he did.

She could say nothing. Not only because she physically couldn't, for her blindness had now evolved into muteness, but also because she just couldn't pass up this opportunity. This might be her only opportunity in life to see such a godlike man derobe (to any extent) for her viewing pleasure.

She should avert her eyes. She should definitely not study the water drops sluicing down his rippling chest. And she could most certainly not gauge the size of his biceps as he swung his jacket, cravat, and–gulp–waistcoat, on a low hanging branch. If she were any kind of lady, she would not memorize the gripping muscles of his back as he turned to take in the sun.

She was a lady. But in this moment she felt like far too much of a woman to compare.

She needed to get a hold of herself. But his bottom was right there in front of her to squeeze–study! Study! What in the name of science was wrong with her?

And then he turned around, and by god, she thought she might need to take up a new science. Observing and tracking the weather was one thing...

But as he stood in front of her, pants soaked, clinging to all his...bulges, she could see the outline of everything. Her nipples tingled. Her core vibrated with intention.

She flung her chin up and found him staring at her. Had he just caught her staring at his...manhood?

Thank God she was not one to blush.

"Are you all right, Lady...?"

He waited. Again.

She stood frozen. Maybe if she said nothing he would just grab his clothes and disappear. Forever. Except from her mind. Yes, that image, the full three hundred and sixty degrees, was etched into her mind.

"Would you tell me your name?"

But no. He had to go and ask her a simple question like that. "Giselle."

When she added nothing, he filled the silence. "It's a pleasure to meet you." That smile again. That radiance. Who did he think he was? "I'm Felix."

Of course his name was Felix. Like feline. Like a smooth cat stalking his prey. Though what kind of cat stalked prey like her?

And then the cat pounced. Not in any way she could have predicted. No, nothing about his man was what she could have predicted. He pounced by asking, "Would you like to fly a kite?"

***

GISELLE WAS BEAUTIFUL. THE most beautiful woman he had ever seen. And perhaps the most charming. She seemed to have no clue how gorgeous she was. And she was on edge. He could tell. But he could soften her up. If anyone could, he could.

Kite flying would be the perfect–

"Doesn't that seem a bit...unproductive?"

Oh yes, he could soften her up. "I'm so glad you asked that. Though some people might think kite flying is a waste of time, I view it differently. It's the perfect way to empty one's mind."

"Why would someone want an empty mind?"

"You can only fill something that has space to be filled."

He watched as her eyes flicked downward in thought. Then upward. Then downward again.

"I suppose that's true."

"What are you taking notes about?"

She glanced back at the notebook he had seen her scribbling in earlier. It was a stall. But it was futile. "The weather."

Those two words conceded a small turn in his favor.

"You're documenting the weather?"

"Yes." She looked back again at the notebook. When she returned her eyes to him, he knew he had inched his way in. "I submit my findings for Farmers Almanacs."

"So this isn't just a hobby?"

"Indeed, it is not."

"You must be good at it."

"I am."

And just before he could start to doubt himself, she added, "And you..." She pointed to the kite. "Are you good at flying kites?"

The grin that wouldn't leave him alone, plastered itself on his face again. "I am. As good as one can be, I suppose."

He unwrapped the string and held the kite out from his body. Leaving the shelter of the tree, he called out, "Follow me. I'll show y ou."

With a few quick steps he had the kite flying high in the air.

"So this is what you like to do?"

"I love to do this. It's the perfect way to spend an afternoon. Lost in thought. Open to anything."

Giselle was eyeing the kite, curious but skeptical. "What do you think about?"

It was a direct question, and he hadn't been expecting it. "I think about life." He shrugged. "Anything. Everything." But the answer even left him unsettled. "I think about what I want to do in the f uture."

"And what do you want to do?"

"I don't know yet..." He noticed a flicker of a thought cross her face, but he couldn't recognize it. "Do you know what you want to do?"

"I'm surprised you would ask that. I'm a lady. My future is more or less told to me by others, wouldn't you think?"

"No, I don't think that. It might be unconventional, but I think women should have more say in their futures." He pointed to her notebook. "And actually, I think you just might be the unconventional type. So, I'd like to ask again: What do you want for your future?"

The question was too direct. It was too intimate. They didn't know each other and he was asking her about her hopes and dreams. But...it seemed like the most natural thing to ask her. And she answered in the most natural way.

"I want to be a meteorologist."

The kite dipped as Felix let the line slack. "Now that's something." He whistled.

"You think it's too ambitious for a woman?"

"I think it's the right amount of ambition for you."

She stiffened. "What is that supposed to mean?"

"It means I'm impressed that you're so confident. You know what you want out of life. I'm still searching for that. I wish I knew what I wanted. And even more to the point, I think you can have whatever you want out of life."

Chapter 5

"I THINK I WANT to fly that kite." The words were out of her mouth before she could process them. It was so unlike her to be impulsive and...whimsical.

But the whimsy was worth it, if only to see Felix's majestic smile again. That grin...it made her insides quiver. Was that the very explanation for giddiness?

"Here. Take this." Felix held out the kite winder for her to hold. The string of the kite was wrapped around a small rod.

"What if I drop it?"

"You won't."

"How do you know?"

"Here." Felix took a step closer to her. He was in her space. Space where no man had gone before. But...it felt nice. Hot and heavy. But...actually not really nice at all. It felt exhilarating, which was most confusing.

And then the winder was in her hands. And her hands were in his hands. His soft, smooth, long-fingered hands. Masculinity at its finest. His chest bumped her shoulder. She didn't move away from it. She wouldn't admit to leaning into it...but if pressed she might capitulate and confess. She could feel him staring at her profile. She dared not look. Then, he was winding two loops of the string around her wrist. His once smooth voice came out husky, "This should help."

She turned only her head, for fear if she turned her body she might be too drawn into him.

"My father used to do this for us when we were younger." He was still close.

"That seems very trusting."

"That's very intuitive of you. He was a very trusting man. Open. Honest. Kind. Always patient. And usually smiling about something."

"I'm not very intuitive."

"Hmm...well, perhaps it was a lucky guess."

"I don't guess."

Felix chuckled. "What would you call it then?"

"A conclusion. You told me he tied the string around your wrist. I envisioned it. It made me think that he was someone who trusted his children. He wanted you to be independent enough to fly the kite, but he didn't set you up for failure."

"He was a good man," Felix mumbled.

The conversation was too deep. Too intimate. She didn't know this man, yet she now knew something about his father that made her feel closer to Felix. Giselle took a step away from the deep-talking, heat-emanating man.

"You're a natural."

The words flooded her soul. It was hard to believe that the small praise could affect her so much. She turned her eyes to the kite. To the sky. The sky was her happy place. Identifying the clouds lightened her heart. Almost as if she felt like a cloud, just watching them.

"Do you see those cumulus clouds?"

"Cumulus? Clouds have names?"

"Yes. Well, types of clouds have names. It's a fairly recent development. But there are high, medium, and low clouds. Depending on how far above the earth they are. And depending on their shape, they have names. Cumulus clouds are puffy and look like a head of cauliflower. Nimbus clouds are rain-bearing. The wispy clouds are called cirrus. And flat, smooth clouds are called stratus."

"Which ones are your favorite?"

"No one has ever asked me that before."

"Well, surely you must have given it some thought."

"Not really."

"Which clouds do you first look for in the sky?"

"Cumulus."

"Which clouds, when not in the sky, leave you disappointed?"

"I would have to say cumulus."

"So like a good girl, you like your vegetables."

"What's your favorite cloud?" she returned the question.

"Rain clouds. I guess...nimbus. I love the rain. It's an enlivening reset."

Giselle turned back to observe Felix. In this moment, with his questions and answers, he was rivaling the clouds for her attention.

No one had asked her these kinds of questions before. No one had shown any real interest in her discussion of clouds. It was partly why she rarely discussed them anymore. So in hindsight, it surprised her that she mentioned anything at all about the types of clouds. Perhaps there was something comfortable about Felix that led her to share.

To her amazement, any feelings of comfort were obliterated in a sudden gust of wind. The string tugged on her wrist, and the wind yanked the kite toward the pond. They were nowhere near the water's edge, thankfully, but she could feel her feet getting caught in her skirts. She was going to fall. Her heart flooded her body with excessive pumping. Her hands grew sweaty. Her legs tightened. She couldn't stop herself. The kite tugged again. Where had that wind come from? It didn't matter. It was here, and it was threatening to pull her away.

"Steady," a calm voice behind her said. "I've got you." He had one arm tightened around her ribs to keep her from falling, and one hand was grasping the winder to protect her wrist.

But what the dickens was going to protect her heart?

Its pounding was incessant. Fear. Intoxication. Curiosity. Wantonness. She was wrapped around and tied in strings of emotions she had never felt before, and certainly not all together. Her back rested against his still damp chest. She could feel her bottom nestled against his thighs. And that thick, corded arm that was wrapped around her ribs had slid up so that her breasts were now resting atop a man's forearm. Her brain exploded. Darkness.

She thought she had died. All right, not died. She knew she had swooned. But she had never expected that of herself. It wasn't the yanking of the kite, it was the yanking of her heart to the man currently holding her up.

Oh yes, and speaking to her.

"Giselle?" That latched arm pulled tighter around her. Her breasts grew heavy as her nipples tightened.

"Giselle? Are you all right?" He turned her body to face him. But that was the wrong description. Her body didn't face him. Her body molded into his. Her breasts were pressed against his chest, and she stood between his legs. The heat was almost unbearable except she knew it was the only thing she wanted. And she felt completely wanton.

This was her moment. A wallflower in the everloving arms of a god. The chances of this ever happening were so beyond slim that she had never once considered it. Which meant that she had also never given any thought as to what she would do in this situation.

So it was with utter recklessness, impulsivity, and whimsy (everything that she wasn't), that she said, "Kiss me, Felix."

Apparently the god didn't need any convincing. His lips crashed down on hers.

For her first kiss, she would have expected gentleness. A soft graze. A breath of a kiss. But this kiss stole her breath. It was primal. The god had gone feral. It only made sense with him being feline-like. He was a predator, and he had snagged his prey.

She didn't mind one bit.

His lips parted, "Open for me, my beautiful Giselle." It was half demand, half plea. The sound of which stroked through her and stoked a fire in her heart. She threw her arms around his neck, one hand still attached to the kite, by two loops of string. The kite high in the sky, her heart soaring alongside it. She stole back her breath and her one chance at a kiss like this.

Pure instinct took over. That, and her observational nature. What he did, she mirrored. He swept his tongue into her mouth and liquid fire swelled at the juncture between her legs. He must have known about said fire because he reached down and picked her up by the waist.

"Wrap your legs around me," he murmured into her neck.

God, he didn't need to ask her again. She pulled up her skirts, latched onto his hips with her thighs, and tucked one ankle over the other. Her core was pressed to his stomach. And she ached to rub herself all over him.

With his head looking over her shoulder, he pulled them back under the shelter of the tree.

"The kite. It might get stuck in the tree."

"What kite?" Felix grinned at her. Then he leaned his shoulders against the tree trunk, His hands on her hips he slid her core down to rest against his own knotted wood.

As Giselle slid over the bulge, she moaned. A sound she had neither produced nor imagined she could produce.

"Felix," she had to say his name. It made it real.

"Tell me to stop."

"Don't stop."

"But just tell me to stop if you ever need to stop. I'll stop."

"Don't stop," she commanded.

His mouth found her neck. Her neck found meaning for the first time in its life.

His tongue traced her jaw and she moaned his name again. Movement from his arousal enticed her. She was causing this reaction in him. It was a heady sensation, one she couldn't decipher in the moment. All she knew was that she needed his shaft at her center. Again. And probably a few more times after that.

She rubbed herself over him. The friction from his breeches tormenting her. His mouth was all over her face, her lips, her jaw, her neck. His hands braced on her hips.

"God, Giselle, I want you."

She couldn't respond to that. Her heart and head were at odds. Only her body saw a clear path of desire.

"Trust me," he mumbled. "Can you trust me?"

"Yes," she breathed into his hair.

One hand braced under her bottom, the other slid under her skirts. Slowly up her leg, across her thigh, in between her folds. And then holy of holies, his thumb found a tiny, untouched, bud of a spot.

"You're so hot, Gislle. You're on fire."

His words only emboldened her. She nipped at his neck and then brought her mouth back to his. "Open for me," she said.

"Uhhh..."

She didn't know what she was doing, but her body craved his. They groaned together. While his thumb was making small circles, she slid over the bulge in his breeches.

And then it was as if the nimbus clouds were coming in. One atop the other. Heavier. Heavier. And heavier. Darker. Darker. Black. Then rain. It poured over her. Through her. Out of her. It drenched her. Body and soul.

And something must have drench his thumb because he took it and put it in his mouth. Leaving it in his mouth, he rested his head against the tree trunk and grimaced. His face tightened and went slack.

Eyes still closed, he sighed, "Oh my God, Giselle. What have you done to me?"

What had she done to him? She wasn't sure. But the once hard bulge was now soft, and the tiniest movement from her caused him to wince. Equally, perhaps even more importantly, what had she done to herself?

She was ruined. And nobody knew it but her.

Chapter 6

LOVE AT FIRST SIGHT. Love at first kite flying. Love at first release in his pants. Felix didn't know what to make of what just happened.

But if there was one thing he was sure of, it was that Giselle would retreat if he told her that he loved her. For that reason alone, he didn't say anything about his feelings after their moment against the tree. He knew he wanted to marry her. But he was hoping for a love match, just like his parents had experienced together.

Within a second, he made a roughshod plan. Give her a couple of days to fall in love with him, and then ask her to marry him. Then hope with all hope that this was the woman fate had picked out for him.

And if she wasn't...well, fate could go fly her own kite.

Given that it was a roughshod plan, the rest of the day passed without Felix being able to see Giselle alone again. He saw her briefly at dinner, but then she spent the rest of the evening surrounded by friends. His sister had even followed her out of the parlor, foreseeably to visit with her in her room. In the room Felix wanted to be in. He would have to wait.

The next day, Felix told Evan, his twin, about being in love. Evan had taken it in stride, though oddly enough had pressed him to tell an old friend about his plans. They were brothers. Evan should be congratulating him, not trying to convince him to tell his friend, Felicity, about Giselle. Felicity would get the news with the rest of his friends. There was no way he was telling Felicity of his plans before he had even given time to Giselle to fall in love with him.

The conversation with Evan had left him a little rattled, so instead of going to the three-legged race like he said he was going to do, he forgot about it entirely. Instead, he was wrapped up in his own thoughts. Of Giselle and the kite.

And then it came to him. He had an idea for his future. Just an idea, but finally...an idea.

He wrote up a list of all the supplies he would need, and then he had it delivered. Surely the packages would arrive by this evening.

The packages surprised him. They came late that afternoon. Carriages of them. There was no hiding them. Well, there was no hiding the fact that he had packages, but he was doing his utmost to keep the contents under wraps. Literally.

He heard some whispers. But he ignored them. In fact, he ignored everyone for the rest of the day and took his supplies to a workshop on the grounds. And that's where he made his future.

***

WHY WAS FELIX IGNORING her? It shouldn't have hurt. It should have been expected. It was expected. Until it wasn't. Until that kiss. Until the clouds had rained down on her, bathing her anew. She wasn't the type of girl to pine over some wastrel who spent his days flying kites and didn't know what to do with his life. Mostly, she wasn't that kind of girl because she had never been given the chance to truly pine over anyone. Her heart had never leapt into her throat and sunk to her toes in the same instant before.

But then Felix had to come along. With his dark wavy hair, glittering pearls for a smile, and sea blue eyes. She hated his smile. She wanted to hate his smile. She wanted to want to hate his smile.

As far as she knew, the man was holed up in some workshop with packages upon packages. It was obvious to everyone that he had dropped a good weight of pounds on the parcels that had arrived in several carriages. But to Giselle, there was a more prominent picture. Clearly, he was avoiding her. The thought deflated her spirits. It was a cloudless and windfree stratosphere surrounding the heart.

And this was the perfect excuse to relegate him back to just being another one of her predictions.

She wanted to kick herself. She knew men like that weren't interested in women like her. And she wasn't–or more truthfully, didn't have to be–interested in men like him. He was just throwing money around as though he had it to waste. And time? He was just sitting around wasting his time doing whatever it is a man could do in a shack with loads of supplies. What less could she want in a man?

A whole lot less. But she couldn't admit that to herself.

What she could admit was that she was in a terrible mood and a mere glance at her countenance would deter even the cheeriest of souls from approaching her. For that reason, she remained in her room for the evening.

And then came the knock. Well, the second knock, actually. She had expected at least one in the evening, and was not disappointed. Hope had stopped by earlier to check in on her. Surely she wasn't checking in on her again, and at this time of night. It was far too soon since her last check and far too late in the evening for her to come by.

Giselle was already in her nightrail. Had already plaited her hair. She walked over to the door and opened it a crack.

There stood the man she wanted not to want to be there.

"Felix."

"Giselle," he beamed at her as if the whole day had not passed with her fuming at him. "Let me in. Quickly. Before someone sees me out here."

All common sense from all generations past dictated that she close the door. All rational thought from all schools of scientific thinking warned her not to make the same mistake twice.

But then…there was his smile.

And her heart took off into the clouds like a damn kite.

She opened the door, and he squeezed in.

"I needed to see you. We had no time alone today."

"You think you can just call on me anytime and I'll drop what I'm doing for you?"

"Oh," he glanced guilelessly around the room. "I apologize. What am I interrupting?"

"Things," she stammered. She saw her notebook lying on her desk and walked toward it. It was likely the most bacon brained thing she could have done, but she picked it up anyway.

He raised a brow at her, recognizing the book. "Do you cloud watch at night as well?"

She couldn't tell if he was teasing, and she was flustered. So she mumbled something completely sensical, like, "The weather doesn't sleep."

"It doesn't!" He whispered, excitedly. "And I'm not sure I can sleep either. I have the most exciting surprise for tomorrow."

His elation was contagious. She wanted to resist, but it was futile. "What are you so excited about?"

"I can't tell you."

She crossed her arms, still clinging to her notebook. Her lifeline. He strode over to her and grasped her upper arms. His hands were warm, comforting, thrilling. He was abuzz with energy, and it was seeping into her.

"I want to show you tomorrow. I think you'll love it." His gaze penetrated her. "I know I love it already."

And as imperceptive as she was, even she could interpret a deeper meaning behind his words. His confession astounded her. There was no way for him to feel this way about her in such a short time. Yet...if she was really being honest with herself, she was feeling some kind of way about him too.

"You couldn't possibly know how you feel about something before you try it."

"You can," he stepped closer to her. "And I do."

She shook her head.

"I already know. But I would love to try more..."

The sentence hung like a cauliflower-shaped cloud in the air. Full. With startling contrast.

"You're the most beautiful woman I've ever seen–"

"Stop."

"What?"

"That is patently untrue."

He scoffed. "Wait. How can you tell me what is true of my experience?"

"No one has ever called me beautiful before. I know I'm not beautiful."

"You're–"

"Don't lie to me, Felix. I'm average. And I accept it."

"Darling," he pulled her close. "You are the least average person I know." He whispered into her hair. "You're an incomparable. No one has your combination of intelligence, drive, and physical beauty."

"I'm not beautiful."

He laughed. "I was so distracted by your beauty that I fell into a pond. Now tell me that's not beautiful."

Her body stiffened. That's why he fell into the water? That made no sense–

"And don't tell me it doesn't make sense. My eyes saw you. I was captivated by you. I had to know you. And then we spoke, and I was l ost."

As tight as her body was, she felt his sigh. It softened him against her. His voice dropped low, "I promised myself I would wait. I promised myself I would give you time. But I can't. I can't contain it. I have to tell you."

He pulled away from her, and she expected the worst. Her heart slammed into the ground. Her shoulders sunk. He took the notebook from her trembling fingers and placed it back on the table next to her barometer. Looking her in the eyes, he said three words. She never knew until that moment just how much her heart longed to hear those words from a man like him.

"I love you."

But he wasn't done.

"And I'm going to stay with you for as long as it takes until you love me too." And then he dropped the real bomb, "And when you do, I'm going to ask you to marry me."

She gasped. He took it as a sign to kiss her. She didn't complain.

The kiss was soft but searing. It was a plea. A promise. A commitment. He thought she was beautiful, mind and body. He was offering himself to her without the guarantee of something in return. He didn't even know that she loved him, but he was willing to wait.

Well, truth be told, she was not willing to wait.

Chapter 7

"MAKE LOVE TO ME, Felix."

Those were some words. Felix felt as though he could breathe. He had intended to give her more time, but his heart had other plans. Of course, he longed to hear more, but if that's all she could say at the moment, then he could wait. For the words. Not her body. She was asking him to make love to her, how the hell was he going to refuse that?

He picked her up and threw her gently on the bed.

"I would love to take my time with you, Giselle, but–"

"Don't go slow, Felix." There was a wildness in her eyes. Passion. Curiosity. But also...something else.

"I'm not going to change my mind, Giselle. I thought I knew love before, but it was nothing compared to how I feel about you. I'll wait for you. As long as it takes." He could see calmness well up in her eyes. Or were those tears? He leaned down and kissed her temple. "I love you. I'll wait."

She exhaled. And he knew it was an exhale of negative thinking because her body softened. “You don’t need to wait, Felix. I want you. Now. I’ve never done this before. I trust you. Make love to me.”

How many times did the woman need to ask him? Apparently more than once. But she wouldn’t have to say it again. He pulled off his jacket. Loosened his cravat and tugged it down his chest. Off came the waistcoat. And she was watching his every move from her seat against the headboard. He moved slowly to the buttons on his shirt. As her eyes widened, he moved even slower. Her lips parted.

Kneeling, he inched closer to her until he was straddling her thighs. “Undress me, Giselle.” With a slight quiver, she reached up and began to undo his buttons. She gasped when the first one came undone and his shirt fell open to reveal a small section of his chest. Quickly, she unbuttoned the rest, and he pulled his shirt overhead. After throwing it on the floor, he took her hand in his and placed it over his heart.

“You’re my beacon, Giselle. You brought a light into my life that I didn’t even know was missing. You’re the wind and the clouds. You’ve stirred something up in me that can never settle.”

He saw a tear spill from the corner of her eyes. He gently brushed it away with his thumb. She was not a woman of very many words, but he understood her. Even though she couldn’t express what she was feeling, he could feel it inside of himself. He knew. And it was enough. “I want to talk with you every day. Watch the clouds with you. Learn more from you and about you. But mostly, I’d like to fly kites with you in cloudful skies. Every day that we can. Would you like that?”

She nodded.

It was more than enough.

He let a few moments pass before asking, “Do you still want to...?”

“Yes,” she finally spoke. “Um...can you...take those off?” She pointed at his breeches.

"Why yes, yes I can." He stood up and dropped his breeches, fully naked before her. It only made sense that he was the one to be fully open, fully available to her. He wanted her to be comfortable and come to him (and with him) in her own time.

But...as he stood there, erection jutting out near head level, he wondered at how comfortable she actually was.

He didn't need to wait long for his answer. Her eyes were as wide as a tea cup as she stared at him.

It only made him grow thicker and longer.

"Can I...?" She said as she kneeled before him. She was already reaching out a hand. Lightning coursed through him when she touched him. It was so soft, so delicate, even a bit cool. He couldn't help it, but he arched toward her.

Looking up at him through dark lashes, now grasping his shaft, she said, "You're going to think I'm crazy, Felix."

He held back a groan. The pleasure was too much. "Nothing's crazy in here. Between us. Do what feels good. Do what you want. Remember what I told you? You can have whatever you want, Giselle."

She paused. And swallowed. God he watched her swallow with his cock two inches from her face. He hardly heard the whisper over the blood rushing to his head. Both heads. "It looks like a stick of candy."

And then he did groan.

"Can I...taste it?"

With another groan, Felix reached for one of the bed posters before collapsing from the shock and the pleasure. He couldn't answer her, she had already leaned forward and licked him.

He was dripping out of his cock, and she had licked him. He was not going to make it two minutes.

"Giselle, God, you are my delight. You will be my life. But if I don't stop you, this won't last long enough for me to give you pleasure."

She took him in her mouth and hummed. She sucked on him as if he were candy. He was going to explode in her mouth.

He couldn't do that to her as one of her first experiences.

"Giselle," he pulled back. "Let me give you pleasure."

Her eyes half lidded, he undid her robe and then pulled her nigh-trail over her head.

"Beautiful," he whispered.

He settled over her on the bed. As he gazed into her eyes, he slipped a finger along her petals. "God, you're so wet. I think you're ready for me ."

"I know I'm ready for you. I just didn't know until now." She spread her legs for him. Trusting. Opening.

"If there's any pain, I can stop. Just tell me."

She nodded.

Slowly, he eased himself between her and ran his dripping cock over her rain cloud. Her moans told him what he needed to know. And he inched himself into her. Feeling the intense heat, the moisture, and then the clasp. She tightened around him, drawing him in.

Her hips lifted off the bed and she started to move, to take him further inside of her. To ease him out and then back in. Her eyes were closed, and her arms were sprawled out to the side. He thought she was at rest until he saw her gripping the sheets.

"Felix," she called to him. "I don't know what I'm doing."

"You're doing it perfectly."

"I need you."

"I'm right here." He thrust into her, causing a moan.

"I need that."

He thrust again. And again, until she was an endless source of moans and small whimpers. Her body was calling to him as much as his was calling to hers.

"I can feel you tightening around my cock, Giselle." Another moan. "Draw me in, Darling. And when you feel you can't tighten anymore, just let go. Let it all go."

Her walls were gripping him so tightly, he knew he had to garner every once of control if he was going to outlast her and give her pleasure.

When she started arching into him, he didn't think he was going to make it. When she pulled his face down into her breasts, he knew he wasn't going to make it. He needed to suck on that temptingly dark nipple. And if he did that, he was done.

It was worth it. He licked. Nipped. And then sucked. Her cry rent the air. The release was singular. He had never been clenched so tightly. Never had his heart wrenched so perfectly. Never had his soul so entrenched so deeply. This was his future.

***

THE NEXT AFTERNOON, FELIX was beyond euphoric. This was the afternoon for the surprise. Everyone from the house party had gathered in the gardens, and Hope, his sister, was leading the event.

"This afternoon's event is kite flying. To make it interesting, you'll each partner up and whoever flies their kite the longest shall receive a small prize."

"Pudding I hope!" A voice called out.

"I'm still waiting for my prize from one of the last events," one of Felix's brothers called out.

Hope's smile quelled the masses, "All will be well. Each person will receive their prize. Not to worry. And it may be pudding. We shall see."

Giselle was standing beside Felix. "You're my partner," he claimed. Her smile tugged on his heart. Or was that the burning in his gut? He was anxious. But he couldn't stop himself. Last night had been perfect. They had made love three times. And they had talked until dawn. He had to slip out of her room and pray he wouldn't be caught. From the conversation, and other things, he knew how she felt about him. Even if she wasn't saying it.

"Felix," Giselle rested a hand on Felix's forearm. "Did you make all of these kites for everyone?"

He grinned sheepishly. He knew she would find out. Probably most of the guests would find out about his small, but kind gesture, even though that wasn't his intent.

"I did."

"That's very kind of you."

"Thank you."

"Why did you do it?"

"I like making kites. I love flying kites. I want to share that joy. You inspired me. I told you that you're my beacon. My nimbus. The very best kind of rain cloud, of course. And I think I know what I want to do. I want to make kites."

He saw her pause, giving consideration to the odd idea. "That's lovely." She smiled at him, and he knew she meant it. Even though he hadn't even explained the entire idea.

"It will be lovely. But it will also be practical. Imagine the possibilities for kites. One day, people might use kites to observe the weather. There's a man in France experimenting with ways to transfer light onto paper. A painting of sorts, but with light. Maybe one day the sky can be captured. Weather might be monitored in new ways. Maybe one day kites will be large enough to carry people into the sky." His ideas were running away from him, and he knew how he sounded. "I know, it sounds crazy–"

"It doesn't sound crazy. It sounds like the future."

"And what an incredible future it will be."

"I can't envision it the way you do, but I'll be there to document it."

He wanted to pull her into his arms and kiss her right there in front of everyone. But he managed to control his arms. And his lips.

"Let's go over there," Felix pointed to a spot in the middle of the garden.

"Dead center is not normally the place I would take."

"You're with me though."

"True. As long as we're together."

That's exactly what he wanted to hear. He took the bridle of the kite and jogged a few paces until it was up flying high in the sky.

He knew he could fly it all day. He had done so on many occasions.

But today was not one of those days. There was no time to waste.

He started reeling the kite back in.

"Felix," Giselle's voice was tied with a small string of panic. "We're going to lose. We need to keep the kite up for as long as possible."

"I can't."

"Of course you can. You're an excellent kite flyer."

"Yes, but there's something wrong with the kite."

"Oh dear."

Felix reeled the kite in. "Can you help me grab it?"

Giselle reached up and took hold of the kite.

"Can you see what's wrong with it?"

"I know nothing about kites."

"Just take a look. Tell me what you see."

He watched her study the kite. Read the kite. Gape at the kite. Hug the kite. Cry into the kite. Then turn to him and throw her arms around him.

"Yes!"

***

Later that day, Giselle stood in front of the mirror in her guest bedchamber. She wiggled the ring around her finger. She was engaged. To a dreamer. Of all men. A handsome, besotted dreamer. How any such man could be besotted with her, she still wasn't sure.

Felix entered her room quietly. "I had to see you."

She smiled at him as he came near. Placing his hands on her hips, he pushed up behind her. His thighs were rubbing against her bottom. Her back rested against his torso. He was strong. Warm. Happy. An incredibly heady combination. She locked eyes with him in the mirror.

"I love you," she blurted out.

His smile radiated at her. "I'm so happy to hear you say those words."

"I do love you. Though, I'm still not sure why you think I'm so beautiful. I think we should marry quickly so you don't change your mind."

Felix's chuckle rumbled against her shoulder blades. "Maybe one day you'll see what I see," he whispered into her ear.

She looked at herself in the mirror. Her blonde hair was pinned back, and a few pieces hung loosely around her face. Her cheeks were slightly rosy. She knew she was intelligent. She was pretty sure she was kind hearted. And now she was, apparently, lovable. More importantly, she was loving. Perhaps, she was beautiful.

***

Giles has to look out for his best mate's sister. That shouldn't have involved kissing her. Can Giles shake the guilt he feels for overstepping his role as protector? Read The Spy and the Spinster to find out!

***

Wondering about other strong, smart women taking their destiny into their hands? Claim your free copy of Sweeten the Rogue when you sign up for Eliana's newsletter to see how Elisa saves her family from ruin.

Second Author's Note

This is the first time I'm adding an author's note about my writing process. I loved writing Giselle and Felix's story.

I love a happy man. Haha

And I love a smart woman. Even more. (Maybe? Haha Equally)

The combination ran deep for me. I had to cut a lot out. But I endeavored to capture her overthinking underspeaking nature as well as his open hearted optimism.

I could have gone down so many rabbit holes of research, but since this is a short book, I had to cut my research in the bud. I looked into clouds, meteorologists, barometers, kites, weather patterns in England, early photography, flying, and so much more. Obviously very little made it into the story, but all the same, I tried to provide some fun little tidbits.

Maybe I'm admitting to major philosophical nerdhood here, but I absolutely adore cloud gazing. It rivals stargazing for me. Do I have a favorite cloud? Maybe cumulus...maybe cirrus...ask me again tomorrow ;) It might change.

Anyways, Giselle is near and dear to my heart. She's an intelligent woman who can't see her own beauty. I feel so many women think this way. And I just want to say, we are ALL beautiful!

The most beautiful thing about a person is their soul. What's in their heart. Giselle is beautiful physically and internally. She is not resentful or bitter. She accepts who she is.

And Felix has one of the happiest, most beautiful souls I've written. I could have gone so much deeper with him too, alas, this is a short book. And this story was actually already longer than the first five in the series. Sooo... that's saying something.

At this point, I'm rambling, but I just want to reiterate. Know your beauty, inside and out. No matter how old you grow. You are beautiful. In fact, I would venture to say that if you are learning and growing, you are more beautiful today than yesterday.

Beauty is not something that belongs to the youth. Beauty only grows deeper and more profound as we age because only as we age do we truly understand the meaning, the impact, the source, of beauty.

Thank you for reading, Beau Monde!

Stay Connected

Please leave me a review :)

If you like my books, please leave me a review. You can find my books through my Amazon Author page here.

https://amazon.com/author/elianapiers

Leaving a review and sharing on social media are the best ways to show love to an author.

Find me and follow me online:

1. My Facebook READER GROUP: Eliana Piers' Beau Monde Reader Groupto hear from me directly and get the inside scoop on what I'm writing. (Readers here also sometimes have input into my upcoming stories.)

2. My Facebook Page: www.facebook.com/elianapiers

3. Instagram: @ElianaPiersAuthor

4. Bookbub: https://www.bookbub.com/authors/eliana-piers

5. Tiktok: ElianaPiers

Read a FREE eBook:

Get my **FREE** book when you sign up to join my mailing list. Plus you'll learn more about me, get sneak peeks at what's in the works, as well as access to some discounted or free books from other authors.

Sweeten the Rogue: One wager, one evening of passion, two possible futures for a rogue and a lady

https://bit.ly/SweetenTheRogue

ARC Team:

If you love my books, want to review them, and share them on social media, then you can sign up to see if you're eligible to join my ARC team to receive FREE advanced copies. *Limited spots available.*

http://bit.ly/ElianaPiersARCForm

Thank You

Thanks Dad. The KITE scene!!! YES!

Thank you to my beta readers, Jenni Simonis and Jordan Lynch. You are the best!

Thank you Staci for your incredible feedback :D

Thank you to all my ARCs. I'm soooo soooo sooo glad you're all enjoying this series.

Thank you to my loving husband. Maybe we should go fly a kite...

Thank you to you, my *beau monde*! You nearly all chose Evan or Felix (the grump over the optimist...) what say you now? haha maybe the same...? maybe both...? haha Oh, my first twins. They were fun to write.

Much love!

About the Author

Eliana Piers, award-winning and best-selling author, has been writing and singing stories since she was five years old. After feeling inspired by authors like Julia Quinn, Tessa Dare, and Minerva Spencer, Eliana decided to test her quill on the page.

Writing about love and how two people come to connect and share parts of their souls with each other is now an obsession.

It's not worth it if you don't laugh, learn, or love while you're in it.

Eliana lives in Canada where she drinks an ice cap every day.

Also By Eliana Piers

Side Stories

Sweeten the Rogue (Novelette)

The Rogue and the Reader (Novelette)

The Good Dukes Series

Good Duke Gone Cold

Good Duke Gone Hard

Good Duke Gone Bad

Good Duke Gone Low

Good Duke Gone Far

Good Duke Gone Rogue

Coming soon (2024): Good Duke Gone Wild

Dukes for Christmas Fairytale series

A Beauty for a Duke

An Ember for a Duke

A Slumber for a Duke

MORE to COME in 2024!

The Ashbourne Legacy series

The Blighter and the Bluestocking

The Scoundrel and the Scientist

The Virgin and the Vixen

The Rogue and the Rose

The Rake and the Writer

The Wastrel and the Wallflower

The Spy and the Spinster

Read More Ashbourne Brothers

Turn the page for more in The Ashbourne Legacy series.

The Spy and the Spinster

1816 England

IT WAS AN ODD feeling to sense being watched. Not *watched* as in observed across a crowded room. Not *watched* as in on a stage or completing a performance of some kind. But *watched* as in, the person watching was hiding, and the person being watched couldn't see them. That was what was odd.

It could almost be frightening except for two things, Lady Hali Collins, the Duke of Tinsder's sister, did not scare easily, and two, Hali knew exactly who was watching her. He was not as discreet as he hoped to be. Oh, she had known the first time it occurred, too. She had been out for a solitary walk in the gardens when she sensed being watched.

When she casually turned to survey the landscape, she saw him. Him! Just watching her. He had pressed himself up behind a tree, but he was much wider than the tree. She almost laughed out loud, but then she thought of why he might be following her. If she laughed, she would give away that she was on to him. So instead, she kept her secret and devised a trick of her own.

Her first test was to meander through the garden, retracing her steps, overlapping her tracks, and then doubling and tripling back. Sure enough, he followed. She had even heard a few overwrought sighs a time or two. Certainly those made it difficult to contain her amusement, but now she had a mission. First and foremost, she wanted to see just how far she could push him to follow her. For example, would he follow her if she waded through the pond? Would he climb a tree? Would he lay in the fields to refrain from being seen? There were so many possibilities. Endless in fact. Secondly, and probably more importantly, she needed to ascertain his motivation in spying on her.

So here she stood, midnight, in the library of Snowick Abbey where she was a guest for a house party. Tempting fate. Tempting her observer. Would he follow her into the library at midnight? If so, how did he know she was there? And wasn't he concerned for her reputation? And his future?

All of those thoughts trailed through her mind in parallel to her trailing her finger across the spines of the beautiful books on the shelves. She stopped at Pride and Prejudice, tilted it down off the shelf, and flipped open the cover. It was one of her favorite stories. She would read it again tonight, but for now she placed it on the side table for later retrieval.

She shouldn't be reading tonight. It was a house party, and there would be plenty of activities the next day, she was sure. Yet here she was, unable to sleep. Her dear friend, Hope, the youngest daughter in the Ashbourne family, had invited her. But of course, Hope, along with the rest of the guests, were in bed. But not those expected eyes.

Those eyes. She could feel them on her skin. It was all dreadfully peculiar, though strangely protective. Hali was used to feeling peculiar, but for entirely different reasons. She was a spinster, even at four-and-twenty, the whispers had already deemed her long in the tooth. It was all absurd. She felt as though she had plenty of time to get married. Her mind, body, and spirit were still able and ready, should any brave and unaffected souls manage to approach her.

She was also familiar with feeling protected. Michael, her brother the duke, was always on high alert with her. He was the one fending off the fortune hunters who had made countless attempts to wrangle her into a scandal.

Unfortunately, Michael wasn't here. He had had business to attend to.

Yet here she was, alone, but with the same sense of protection. It was Giles after all. The spy, that is. He was Hope's older brother, but the baby of the seven brothers.

There was nothing about Giles to cause concern.

He was...nice. She actually didn't know too much about him. He was one of the only brothers in the Ashbourne family who had avoided dancing with her. In all their years, they hadn't danced together once. It was strange, to say the least.

Stranger still that he was in this room with her. Alone. If anyone caught them, it would cause a scandal. Scandal enough to warrant a marriage proposal.

She could sense him behind the curtains. How he got there, she wasn't sure. But she had seen the curtains swish a few times.

Perhaps she should give him a reason to sweat. She wandered over to the window and pulled back the empty curtain to stare out into the darkness. Looking for stars, she took a step back, nearly brushing up against him.

She dipped her chin and placed her hand over her lips to suppress a chuckle. It was nearly impossible. She would have to leave the room so as not to give herself away. Dashing to the door, without making it an obvious dash, she swung it open and stepped into the hall. She took a deep breath. She had nothing to worry about. It was only Giles.

***

GILES EXHALED LOUDLY. THAT had quite possibly been the worst moment of his life. Pure torture. One hundred percent, fate's vicious vouchsafing him a victim of the friendzone. That was the closest he had been to Hali in a long time. Her body had been inches away, and she had no clue he was there or why.

Hell, he hardly understood why he was there anymore. He tapped the letter in his pocket. The reminder. Michael had sent him the letter requesting that he keep an eye on Hali because there were always fortune hunters after her. Michael trusted him to protect his sister from harm and scandal. So what the blazing ballocks was he doing following her into the library at midnight? Preceded was more truthful.

He had enlisted the help of a footmen and servant or two, so he was always aware of her comings and goings. Once he received word that she was out of her room, he knew she would head for the library, so he took his chances, which were good, and raced there.

Spying on her in the library, though, wasn't that going a bit too far? He could only justify it by thinking that Michael would prefer a possible scandal result in Giles marrying his sister rather than some two-faced coin chaser.

That was what he told himself. And he almost believed it.

But the moment she had nearly backed her bountiful bottom against his bulge, he knew he was in trouble. Again.

He knew it the first time he had laid eyes on her. She was gorgeous. Soft, warm chestnut hair. Eyes to match. But perhaps a shade darker. He had fallen for her the moment he saw her. But the second moment he saw her, he overheard her. And she was telling Michael that she didn't want to marry. Ever.

That and he had no money. So if he did approach her, he knew she would throw him in with the rest of the fortune hunting lot.

So, like every respectable English gentleman, he had bottled up all of his feelings and ignored them.

Then he proceeded to make heaps and heaps of money. For himself, of course. It had nothing to do with her. So he told himself.

And now, with his heaps and heaps of money, and mountaining manhood–and that damn letter and a promise–he was in terrible trouble.

He was worried. Very, very worried.

Read More: Dukes for Christmas

Turn the page for Chapter 1 of Book 1 in the Dukes for Christmas series: *A Beauty for a Duke.*

Beauty with brains meets a big, grumpy Beast just before Christmas. Only a third wheel and a long carriage ride are in their way...

A Beauty for a Duke

Chapter 1

1816, England

JUST ONE MORE CHAPTER. She had to finish just one more chapter. It could easily be done before–

"Sofie," drawled her curvy, and heavy-bosomed friend, Fia. Since childhood the two had been inseparable. What more did they need than for their names to complete each other? Sofie and Fia together since six. Or was it five? It was all the same. They had so many shared memories together that if one forgot, the other was likely to remember. Though, if the truth were being told, and it usually was among the two of them, Fia was the one with the better memory for events. And Sofie was more dependable for remembering ideas. And making plans. Or, more accurately, roping the two of them into haphazardly constructed plans.

Which was exactly how the two had met. It was Sofie's first time going out alone to buy bread for the day. Her father had finally allowed her that small amount of freedom, so she skipped all the way there. When she looked up into the eyes of a small girl about her size, she said, "I must have lost my coins skipping all the way here. Oh no! Papa will never trust me with money again."

The little girl behind the counter replied, "I'll help you find them. That's what friends are for. Papa won't mind, will you Papa?" She swiveled her bouncing crimson curls to her father, the baker, who was already nodding his head.

She darted out from behind the counter saying, "I'm Fia by the way."

"I'm Sofie."

Fia squealed, "Oh, that's perfect! I always wanted my name to be Sofie, and now, together, we shall make the best of friends with the loveliest of names."

Sofie grinned, "We're friends?"

"Why not?"

She couldn't agree more.

"Let's go." And the two girls had pranced off in search of treasure. Not only had they found the coins, but they had also swam with mermaids and fought dragons the entire way. Much to their surprise, they both returned home without a scratch. From that day on, not a day had passed without the two of them seeing each other. They knew all there was to know about the other.

So that's why Fia could easily read Sofie's mind as she stared at the book in front of her.

"I know you are probably convincing yourself that you can squeeze in one more chapter of reading, but really, I can't serve the entire tavern by myself."

Sofie was leaning over her open book, head down, breasts resting on the high table in the backroom of The Crowned Rose, owned by her father, Richard. She tucked a stray chestnut strand behind her ear.

Finally she glanced up to find Fia sliding her hand over her perfectly coiffed crimson hair and then flicking an invisible fleck from her bodice. How she always managed to look so put together and kept up, Sofie couldn't be sure. Sofie was never unkempt, or...unput together, but she could certainly use a few extra pins at any given time.

"Alright, Fia, I'm coming. Just one more page."

The eye that her friend gave her spoke almost as loudly as the din coming from the main room just beyond the door. It must be a full house. *When had that happened?* Last she checked, which could have been hours ago, half of the tables were open. She had even thought to attempt some Christmas decorating after she finished her chapter. Or entire book. Whichever came first.

"Alright, alright. Just let me finish this sentence."

"I'll wait." Fia tapped her foot.

"Done," Sofie placed her paper rose bookmark in between the pages and pushed the book into the large pocket in her frock. To be sure Sofie didn't pull a fast one, Fia threaded her arm through Sofie's, and coaxed her back to work.

Sofie entered the chaos, grateful for the work she had. Being in Derbyshire near the Duke of Somersby's estate, despite its small size, the public house had the pleasure of serving many a patron from England and beyond.

Perhaps not now that Christmas was fast-approaching. Everyone would be tucked away in their warm homes, sidling up to fires and roasting treats. If not now, then at least within the next week. Which meant that within the next seven days, her friend Adeline, Lady's maid to the Duchess of Somersby, would soon pay her and Fia a visit. She usually had a frock or two for each of them that were only a couple of years out of fashion. Fashion didn't matter much to Sofie, though Fia might let a few complaints grumble out of her. They weren't complaints so much as observations. Or so Fia always reminded her.

"Sofie, glad you could make an appearance," her father's eyes shone brightly at her. He was truly the most perfect father she could have ever asked for. Even after her mother had passed away, in spite of his grief, he had done his utmost to run the tavern and take care of Sofie the best way he knew how. In fact, there were several ways they honored her mother, Layla, including the placement of a few roses on the walls and in the guest rooms. The red rose was her mother's favorite.

"I'm here for you, Papa." Sofie patted her father's hand and took notice of the extra wrinkles. He had been working a long time at his dream of running the tavern. She only wished he needn't work quite so hard. The tavern was his life, but she wished it didn't have to be his lifeline.

That's why for the last few years she had convinced him to give her some of their profits to invest. And so far she had earned more money than she had lost. Of course, she had to do some wrangling with solicitors and her father any time she wanted to make any changes, but that little hindrance didn't stop Sofie on her quest. It only precipitated more dreams of the day she could have her own bank account and her own full control of her money. As it so happened, this dream was one of the reasons she didn't want to marry, despite having received several offers over the years. Also, every marriage proposal thus far had been prefaced with something akin to, "In light of your great beauty...etcetera etcetera, will you marry me?" She did not want to be someone's trophy. Nor did she want to be anyone's property. In the event she did marry, any authority she might have gained would then transfer over to her husband. And she did not want to have to ask her husband to sign off on every financial decision she made.

And equal to the point, she was more than the beauty men whispered (or spoke loudly) about. She prided herself (though not overly) on her intelligence. Having spent all her spare time, and some working hours, reading all that she could about investments, it was not a pride without foundation. Besides books, if there were any conversations about interest and profit that she could glean wisdom from, she took the time to serve those tables with extra care.

And there were a few patrons who would come in from time to time reliably with interest-full conversations. Lord Reginald was not one of those few, but if he was ever in attendance with the Colonel or any of his duke friends, Sofie served them well. And aside from a recent, but small, incident with Lord Reginald and his friend, the newest Duke of Beauford, every encounter so far had been well-received.

And so it was that if ever a new patron came in talking of investments, Sofie and Fia confirmed with their eyes who would take the table. Because if Sofie could invest and save enough money, she would not only help her father, but of course her best friend as well.

Now, if only she could find a way to attend the Railway Convention happening tomorrow...But that felt like more of a castle in the air dream than a simple castle in the air itself.

Besides the fact that the logistics were a nightmare, there was also the question of how her father would manage in her absence. How would she travel there? How would she gain entrance? Who would go with her? How would she pay for it?

No, it was not meant to be. Castles did not exist in the air. And tavern daughter's did not attend annual Railway Conventions.

Read more.

Read More: The Good Dukes

Turn the page for Chapter 1 of Book 1 in The Good Dukes series: *Good Duke Gone Cold.*

She's a passionate playwright. He's a grumpy, cold duke. And she just needs to resist her desire for him this one summer...

Good Duke Gone Cold

Chapter 1

1815, England

A GIRL NEVER KNOWS where her husband might come from. He could be the neighbor next door. Down the street. He could be her father's friend. A distant cousin twice removed. He could be an earl, a viscount, a prince. He could be the man she just waltzed with or the one waiting behind the fern working up the nerve to ask for the next dance. Or. Or just maybe he could be the clothesless, dripping wet adonis right in front of her.

The memory was so vivid, it felt like he was right in front of her. But where had that memory come from just now? Maybe it was the rain sluicing down the window. That must be it. Mary shook her head. Now was not the time for that memory.

Now was the time to focus on herself and being more than just a woman waiting for a husband. Now was the time to focus on her desires, namely, writing her first play to be performed in front of an audience other than friends and family.

The blank pages rested heavily on her lap. It was strangely warm and comforting, despite its emptiness. This was the year. No, this was t he *summer* she would finish this play. It's going to happen. It has to happen. Lady Mary Edwards consoled herself as she brushed a loose cinnamon coloured tendril behind her ear. She would be more than just a woman pursuing fleeting beauty and a faulty husband. There must be more. And this play was it.

Her legs were bent as her back rested against the window frame. She was cozy as her slight frame was hidden behind the drapes. Surrounded by books and feeling the faint flickers from the fire soothed her soul into a state of meditation. This was the place to think. To feel inspired. To express all her pent up passions and let all the words flow into glorious being and insurmountable greatness. To look down at a blank page. Well, yes. All in good time. The play was half written but something was missing. If only she could–

Mary shook her head and peered out the window. She didn't stare at the perfectly manicured trees in the shapes of exotic animals in front of her, or even the fountain full of cherubs. Her mind's eye wandered across the ducal fields of her best friend's family home and onward to her own less opulent estates hidden from view, where neither her father nor mother, in fact no family, was currently in residence. Father and mother had left again. This time to excavate the latest Egyptian treasures. Last time was Morocco. The time before that was Tunisia, or was it India? Every few months took them to a new place with the hollow platitude that she would be fine, if not happier, at her best friend's nearly palatial estates. *Two is more fun than one,* they'd say. *We'll see you soon, have fun with Margaret. Be good. Oh what are we saying, of course you'll be good. Try to keep Margaret in line. Her parents love your influence. See, it's a win-win for everyone.*

Mary didn't mind. Too much. It *was* better with two. And Margaret *was* her best friend. Always had been. Ever since Margaret literally ran into Mary in the fields one day with the biggest grin and wildest eyes she had ever seen. The tenacious memory forced its way back to Mary's mind.

She could still remember the cool breeze on her cheeks. Standing in the middle of a pathway, forgetting to take the next step, she lost her thoughts in the clouds. There were shapes of animals and boats scudding across the sky, morphing into flowers and trees. What made the clouds move? Did others see the same shapes? What would it be like to rest on one of those clouds for a day?

Then, thwack! Something, no, someone, had just run into her shoulder.

Without even taking time to introduce herself, the girl–later found out to be Margaret–yelled, "Run! They're coming!" Mary didn't hesitate. This was not a time to consider the pros and cons or the risks of what might be coming out of the bushes. She picked up her skirts and tried to run after the spritely blonde girl who was still shrieking like a banshee.

Unfortunately, Mary was not made for such impulsive moments as this. Lost in the hysterics, she didn't notice the girl in front of her flinging up an armful of clothing. Instead of the odds of just one item hitting Mary, it seemed like all thirteen items hit her right in the face and caused her to trip over a root and fall face first in the dirt.

Her heart was pounding. She heard footsteps racing toward her. What was coming from behind the hill? How many were there? Who had that girl angered? How angry were they? Mary's palms were clammy. She rolled over, getting tangled in the clothing and was pulling pieces of clothing from her eyes as quickly as she could. And then, in an indelible instant, she wished she could put everything back over her e yes.

Looking up, her eyes beheld the wettest, most heart-throttling sight she had ever seen. Water sluiced down the carefully crafted body right before her eyes. Before her own very eyes.

She should have closed them. She should have put her head back under the loose clothing. Every admonishment and warning ever prevailed upon her reminded her to be genteel. A woman was to be prim and proper, yet every fiber in her body refused to obey. Her eyes took their fill. By Jupiter, he was everything her mind could have thought up to be the embodiment of what a man should be. He lifted one of his large hands to push back his luscious raven hair, just long enough to brush the tops of his ears. The action exposed his thickly arched eyebrows that framed piercing azure eyes, an aquiline nose, and a strong sharp jaw.

Her embarrassingly evident perusal was interrupted with an abrupt demand, "Where is she?" Spoken with such aplomb, Mary hardly believed he knew he had one hand covering his, um, other areas. *Oh did I actually look that far down. It's not possible. I am a lady. Well, ten is almost an adolescent and that's nearly an adult. But I am proper.*

"Uh–"

"You don't look familiar. I suppose you don't even know her, do you? *Her* being Lady Campbell, or Margaret, in light of the forced intimacy of this acquaintance. Well, all in good time. Perhaps you'd like to grace us with our belongings currently entangling you?"

At that moment a second rustling in the bushes and a calm, "Jonathon, just wait there for a moment, please," led her to turn on her stomach and rest her closed eyes on her forearm.

Oh please let this be over soon. Please. Please. Please. Please don't tell my mother and father about this. Just let this be a nightmare.

If only Mary knew what a recurring dream this nightmare would turn into, she might have put a little more effort into listening to those clamoring voices earlier, reminding her to be proper and not continue looking in the first place.

"Well, alright. On your stomach then. If you can't see me, then I'm sure I'm not here. Just stay put. I'll reach around you and grab our clothes. We'll dress quickly and this will all feel like a dream."

Nightmare. Dream. Really, what's the difference besides the untrustworthy emotions they evoke.

***

GREGORY CAMPBELL, DUKE OF Wellingford, stood in the front hall dripping wet from the day's showers. This was home. He should feel comfortable. He should be sauntering in, taking charge, and acting like he owned the place. He did own the place.

At the very least he should be getting changed. But he was frozen in place. As he looked at the front door, he couldn't stop thinking about one of the last times he stared at that same door just after slamming it at his best friend's back. He could still hear the angry shouting.

"You don't know anything, Jonathan. You don't know pain. You don't know the real world. You're just the devil may care, everything will work out guy who doesn't think about anything beyond his next meal or his next lay."

Jonathan, like Gregory, was five-and-twenty at the time. But everything else was unlike Gregory. Where Gregory had turned dark, stern, and mysterious after his father passed away, Jonathan was light and transparent. His shoulders were never burdened like Gregory's, and everything that would have weighed on Gregory rolled right off Jonathan's back. Even his caramel colored hair was cropped shorter and styled asymmetrically, as if he needed more proof of his cavalier approach to life.

Unprovokably, Jonathan's lips curved into a half smile. "Yes. That's right. That's me. That's why we're friends. You keep us from getting into too much trouble, and I keep us from being too dainty."

"Dainty?!" Gregory scoffed. "Is that what you call it? Responsibility? Ownership? To hell with you."

"What are you so riled up about? You know me, I'm always joking around."

"Not everything is always a joke."

"Well, this surely is."

"Right now, your life surely is."

And then, the ever unflappable Jonathan, gave his half smile for the second time, saluted Gregory, and walked out the door.

He walked right out the door, enlisted in the army, and never walked through the doors again. All this, on the anniversary of Gregory's father's death.

"Gregory!" The shout pulled him out of his trance. "My brother, the prodigal in the flesh, has returned! I can't believe you are here. It has been far too long."

"Yes, Margaret. It has been." Margaret, Lady Campbell and her turquoise almond shaped eyes was always sporting a coquettish grin.

She flung her arms around his neck. In fact, come to think of it, Margaret flung many things around, including convention and clothing. His younger sister was overly cheerful, albeit spoiled and somewhat meddling. But her love was always genuine. If not a tad dramatic at times. Women.

Gregory had two rules for women. Keep them happy. And keep them at arm's length.

"–and that is the best part! I'm so happy!" Rule one: check.

"Wonderful. Well, it's good to be home." He turned his head to look back at the door. The distressing memory was like a drain. It was pulling him in so much that he didn't even hear the footsteps and further chatter from Margaret until he felt a light thwump against his chest. Immediately his hands reached down encircling the most perfectly sized-waist. He inhaled a familiar, but exotic, scent of cinnamon and vanilla. The lithe body in his hands was warm and soft, everything he stole his heart against. He felt two pert breasts nuzzled against his chest and then two timid tawny eyes met his.

This was Mary. Margaret's little friend who was not so little anymore. She was a hot blooded grown woman pliable in his hands. He had met Mary when she was ten years old, and she and Margaret had followed him and Jonathan around like lost puppies, until they all became friends of a sort. He recalled teaching her how to fish, ride a horse, and parry a blade. They had always been respectful of each other and had always had innocent fun together. So as his hands melted into her waist after three years of not seeing her, it was uncomfortable to have thoughts enter his mind about what he might teach her as an ad ult.

What was he thinking? He didn't need this distraction. He came home with a purpose. Everything had to be about the dukedom now. He'd spent enough years wasting his life away on gambling, women, and alcohol. What was it, two? Three? Now it was time to at least have a semblance of control. If not in direct pursuit of cleaning up his reputation, at least to take on responsibilities and not squander the inheritance his ancestors had carefully built and maintained over the last few hundred years.

Hell, this was Chatswick House accommodating 154 bedrooms, 20,000 acres, and hundreds of tenants. There was plenty of work that needed his attention here. His father would be proud that he had finally returned to take his place and start behaving how he had been trained to act. His father was his greatest ally and staunchest supporter. He knew how far to push Gregory. He knew when to hold back and when to unleash. And then in an instant, at sixteen, he was gone. No more strong, unwavering voice reassuring him of his abilities and pushing him to rise to new challenges.

Always a boy with confidence, Gregory had focus and exactitude suited for being a duke. When his father died, he pushed down the hurt, suppressed the uncertainty, and faced his responsibilities with dignity.

Then, when Jonathan went missing at five-and-twenty, Gregory hadn't held it together as well. In fact, he hadn't held it together at all. Now it had been three years since he'd returned, and it was time to come back. It was time to build a home. He had a three step plan: reassess the estates, throw himself into a hobby to avoid close relationships, and secure a wife. Perfectly sound.

Home... Yes, this was the house he grew up in, but it didn't feel like home anymore. He wasn't sure what home was. He knew he needed a roof over his head to protect his body, he knew he needed a hobby for his time and to fill his mind, and he knew he eventually needed an heir for the dukedom to gain his title.

But right here in his hands was someone who used to feel like home. All the memories they shared together threatened to flood his mind, but then, barely beyond a whisper, he heard, "Your Grace."

***

MARY SLOWLY LIFTED HER delicate hands to Gregory's chest to push herself back. It felt like he wasn't letting her go, but that must have been her imagination. Of course, he wasn't holding on to her. Of course, he wasn't holding his breath.

"Isn't that so like me?" Margaret effused. "Here I go attempting the dramatic entrance by twirling our dear, dear friend, and I accidentally overshoot." Margaret chuckled. Her blonde hair glittered in the light, and her shimmering eyes matched the glow. She was effervescence personified. She was the sparkle to Mary's life. They couldn't be more opposite. Where Margaret would run through fields playing pranks on her brother, Mary had been woolgathering lost in the shapes of the clouds. Once the two met, they were inseparable, and Margaret called to the depths of Mary's soul. Margaret knew immediately of Mary's abstract nature and how her creative soul just needed to be promp ted out.

That's when the plays began. Mary started writing and couldn't stop. Every few months the girls would be reenacting a new play and dragging Gregory and Jonathan into them, only when the boys were home from Eton, that is. And only when they could be cajoled, threatened, or bribed with baked goods, into participating. When not enacting one of Mary's plays, the girls would follow the older two boys, spying on them to see what mischief they could cause.

Of course, this led the girls into learning quite a few things otherwise unbeknownst to girls: how to swim, fish, fence, ride horses, and even shoot. Summers especially, held the most memories for the girls. It all changed drastically a few years ago when Jonathan went missing. There was one less person laughing.

At this moment though, there was only one person chuckling, and it was about the clumsy introduction she had overshot. Margaret was unaware that she was the only one laughing.

Mary noticed, however. She noticed everything at this particular time and in this particular space, including the solid chest, broad shoulders, and the faint scent of bay rum with a hint of whiskey.

This was a solid chest, even more solid than the last time she was plastered against it. That pesky memory fought its way back to her mind, and Mary was transported back to the day they all met.

"Alright, we're both dressed now. You can stand up and open your eyes." Mary lay still on the ground with her eyes pressed into her forearm.

"You've shocked the poor girl," a second voice cheerfully said. "Here. Let me." The voice belonging to Jonathan approached Mary and tapped her lightly on the shoulder. "Come now. Everything is fine. We'll go find your friend and you two can scamper off and continue whatever other shenanigans you had planned for the day."

Mary didn't feel compelled to correct Jonathan that in fact Margaret wasn't her friend, that she never scampered, and she most definitely never engaged in shenanigans. Instead, she thought maybe joining Margaret was the safer bet.

As she lifted her torso from the ground and began to put weight on her foot to get up, she stumbled. "Ack! I believe I may have twisted my ankle." Jonathan was right there and caught her up and into his arms.

"Ooof! Ok hang on. I've got you." But it did not feel at all like he had her. "Let's be off. Hang on tight." And he started to amble down the pathway in hopes of meeting up with Margaret. Mary's head bumped against his chest and her arms were uncomfortably settled on her stomach. Just then, Jonathan tripped and lurched forward. Mary grasped for his neck as he recovered his footing. This did not feel safe at all.

"Darn roots! If I can stumble, being as athletic as I am, I see how anyone could have done so just as easily." His chuckle lightened the mood and put Mary at ease for her earlier stumble, but she was unassured of her current level of safety in his arms.

"Give the chit to me before you break her neck," Gregory demanded with a scowl.

"I'm not a chit! And I'm not just some piece of–" before she could finish Jonathan handed her off Gregory.

"She's all yours! I'm going to find Margaret and give her something to think about." With that he laughed and ran off leaving Mary in Gregory's strong, capable arms, and resting against his solid, warm chest. It was safe, and it felt like home.

That was the moment she fell in love with him.

That solid, warm chest was the same solid, warm chest that she was now resting against. She pulled her mind to the present and pushed herself away from home.

His harsh, cold voice doused her heart with ice water, "Lady Mary."

Read more.

Made in United States
North Haven, CT
18 March 2025

66931868R00050